Little Lies

ALL ABOUT MATH

Written by Kirsten Hall

Illustrated by Bev Luedecke

children's press®

A Division of Scholastic Inc.
New York Toronto London Auckland Sydney
Mexico City New Delhi Hong Kong
Danbury, Connecticut

About the Author

Kirsten Hall, formerly an early-childhood teacher, is a children's book editor in New York City. She has been writing books for children since she was thirteen years old and now has over sixty titles in print.

About the Illustrator

Bev Luedecke enjoys life and nature in Colorado. Her sparkling personality and artistic flair are reflected in her creation of Beastieville, a world filled with lovable Beasties that are sure to delight children of all ages.

Library of Congress Cataloging-in-Publication Data

Hall, Kirsten.
  Little lies : all about math / written by Kirsten Hall ; illustrated
by Bev Luedecke.
    p. cm.
Summary: Slider's friends catch him in a number of lies that add up
until they can no longer trust him.
  ISBN 0-516-22896-X (lib. bdg.)   0-516-24656-9 (pbk.)
  [1. Honesty–Fiction. 2. Trust–Fiction. 3. Friendship–Fiction. 4.
Stories in rhyme.] I. Luedecke, Bev, ill. II. Title.
  PZ8.3.H146Li 2003
  [E]–dc21
                            2003001584

1 2 3 4 5 6 7 8 9 10 R 12 11 10 09 08 07 06 05 04 03

A NOTE TO PARENTS AND TEACHERS

Welcome to the world of the Beasties, where learning is FUN. In each of the charming stories in this series, the Beasties deal with character traits that every child can identify with. Each story reinforces appropriate concept skills for kindergartners and first graders, while simultaneously encouraging problem-solving skills. Following are just a few of the ways that you can help children get the most from this delightful series.

Stories to be read and enjoyed

Encourage children to read the stories aloud. The rhyming verses make them fun to read. Then ask them to think about alternate solutions to some of the problems that the Beasties have faced or to imagine alternative endings. Invite children to think about what they would have done if they were in the story and to recall similar things that have happened to them.

Activities reinforce the learning experience

The activities at the end of the books offer a way for children to put their new skills to work. They complement the story and are designed to help children develop specific skills and build confidence. Use these activities to reinforce skills. But don't stop there. Encourage children to find ways to build on these skills during the course of the day.

Learning opportunities are everywhere

Use this book as a starting point for talking about how we use reading skills or math or social studies concepts in everyday life. When we search for a phone number in the telephone book and scan names in alphabetical order or check a list, we are using reading skills. When we keep score at a baseball game or divide a class into even-numbered teams, we are using math.

The more you can help children see that the skills they are learning in school really do have a place in everyday life, the more they will think of learning as something that is part of their lives, not as a chore to be borne. Plus you will be sending the important message that learning is fun.

Madeline Boskey Olsen, Ph.D.
Developmental Psychologist

Bee-Bop

Puddles

Slider

Wilbur

Pip & Zip

Flippet

Pooky

Mr. Rigby

We're the Beasties

Smudge

Toggles

"Hi there, Slider!" Pooky waves.
"Please come out so we can play!"

Slider shakes his head. "No thanks!
I have other plans today!"

"I am going on a trip!
I will be back very late.

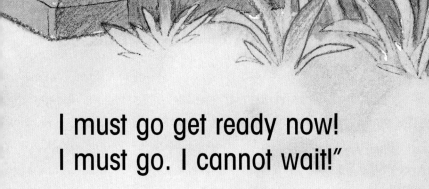

I must go get ready now!
I must go. I cannot wait!"

Pooky finds some other friends.
They are playing. She must hide.

Pooky runs to find a spot.
She sees Slider by her side.

"Slider, why did you not go?"
Slider has nothing to say.

Pooky thinks she understands.
He just did not want to play!

After dinner, Slider rests.
Zip and Pip are at his door.

They ask what he did all day.
"I spent my day at the store!"

"How is that? The store was closed!"
Slider does not know what to say.

He has told a second lie.
Zip and Pip go back to play.

Pooky walks up to the door.
"Slider, have you seen my pie?"

He says no and Pooky frowns.
"Slider, that is your third lie!"

Slider sees his friends outside.
"Hi there! Can I play with you?"

They do not want him to play.
"Nothing that you say is true!"

Smudge sees Slider by the lake.
"Do you have some time to talk?

You look like you need a friend.
Maybe we should take a walk."

"Slider, you told us three lies!
That is why we are so mad.

You should always tell the truth.
Even little lies are bad!"

"Slider, what if I told lies?
What if I told lies to you?

Even telling one is bad.
What you tell us should be true!"

Slider goes to find his friends.
Everyone is still outside.

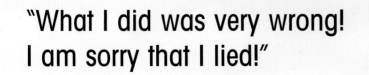

"What I did was very wrong!
I am sorry that I lied!"

BODY COUNT

1. How many Beasties are in this picture?

2. How many stripes do you see on Slider?

3. How many hands can you count?

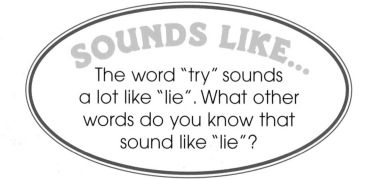

SOUNDS LIKE...

The word "try" sounds
a lot like "lie". What other
words do you know that
sound like "lie"?

LET'S TALK ABOUT IT

1. Why do you think Slider's friends were so mad at him?

2. Is there a difference between a big lie and a little one?

3. Have you ever told a lie? How did it make you feel?

WORD LIST

a	friends	look	seen	to
after	frowns	mad	sees	today
all	get	maybe	shakes	told
always	go	must	she	trip
am	goes	my	should	true
and	going	need	side	truth
are	has	no	Slider	understands
ask	have	not	Smudge	up
at	he	nothing	so	us
back	head	now	some	very
bad	her	on	sorry	wait
be	hi	one	spent	walk
by	hide	other	spot	walks
can	him	out	still	want
cannot	his	outside	store	was
closed	how	pie	take	waves
come	I	Pip	talk	we
day	if	plans	tell	what
did	is	play	telling	why
dinner	just	playing	thanks	will
do	know	please	that	with
does	lake	Pooky	the	wrong
door	late	ready	there	you
even	lie	rests	they	your
everyone	lied	runs	thinks	Zip
find	lies	say	third	
finds	like	says	three	
friend	little	second	time	